rne School

Bradbury Press · New York

WILLIAM
THE
VEHICLE KING

by Laura P. Newton

illustrated by Jacqueline Rogers

Bradbury Press
An Affiliate of Macmillan, Inc.
866 Third Avenue, New York, NY 10022
Collier Macmillan Canada, Inc.
Printed and bound in Japan

10 9 8 7 6 5 4 3 2 1

The text of this book is set in 18 point Century Book Condensed.

Library of Congress Cataloging-in-Publication Data

Newton, Laura P.   William the vehicle king.

Summary: William plays on the rug with a multitude of colorful toy vehicles,
including a sedan like his mother's, a tow truck, and a steamroller.
[1. Vehicles—Fiction. 2. Toys—Fiction]
I. Rogers, Jackie, ill. II. Title.
PZ7.N4868Wi   1987   [E]   86-33412   ISBN 0-02-768230-7

For the past and present Williams in my life,
my father and my son—both vehicle kings

—L.P.N.

To Butch and Todd, true vehicle kings

—J.R.

William needed a car—
a car to hold,
and put in his pocket,
and race along the rug.

He picked out a bright-blue car.

The bright-blue car was wonderful, but

it needed other cars to lead,

and sometimes to follow…

and to race along the rug.

A light-brown sedan just like Mama's was great,

and so was a shiny orange car with a door that opened.

The dark-green van could hold a lot of people, but

the purple racing car held just two.

Soon many cars rode on the rug.

Suppose there was an accident?

William needed a white police cruiser with blue lights
and a long white ambulance with a red light.

He needed a red fire engine
and a sturdy black tow truck, too.

More roads had to be built.

Construction equipment was essential.

William used a dump truck, a grader, and a steamroller.
They were yellow, yellow, yellow.

He worked long and hard building highways.

And when he was through,

cars and trucks went everywhere

with William, the Vehicle King.